Kula...

Kulo...

Kulapa...

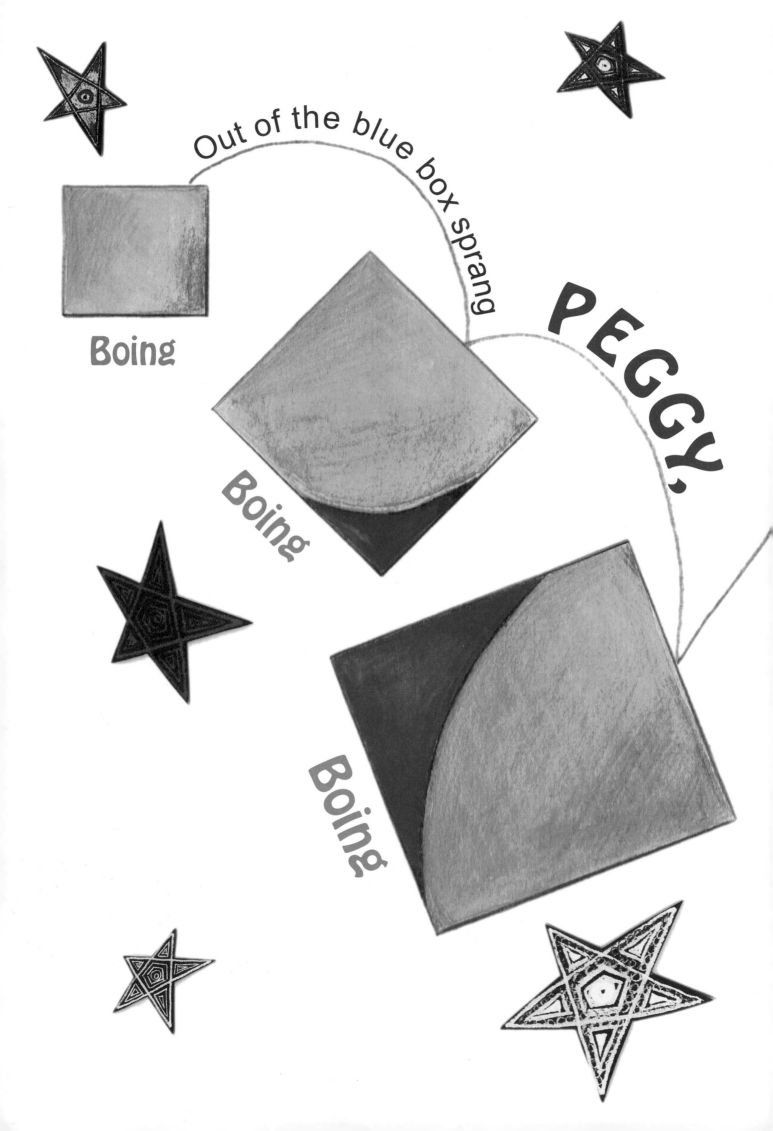

Out of the blue box sprang

PEGGY.

Boing

Boing

Boing

BUDDY
in India

Nazneen Bustani

This book belongs to
the great explorer

BUSTANI

BUDDY, the dog, loves adventures.

He was ready for a new one with best friend Peggy.

Buddy said the magic words...

the magic tent.

"Wow!" said Peggy. "Where are we this time?"

"We're in India," replied Buddy. "Look! There's the Taj Mahal, one of the Wonders of the World."

Buddy and Peggy flew from the World Wonder to Jantar Mantar in Delhi. "Great! An observatory," said Buddy. "These shapes tell the time using the sun."

Later as they hovered over a jungle they heard a tiger's loud...

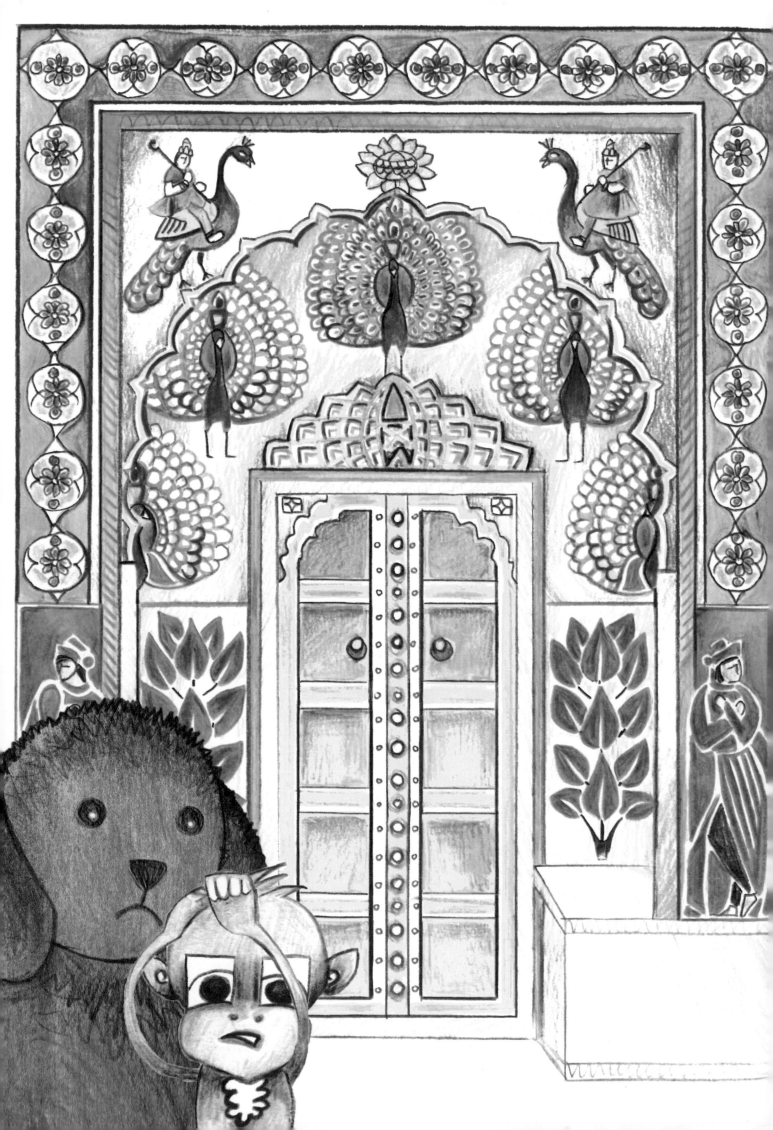

Buddy and Peggy arrived in Jaipur.
They saw a monkey crying near the Peacock Gate.
"Help! Peeku, my best friend has run away,"
sobbed Monkey.
"Where would Peeku go?" comforted Buddy.
"Well, Peeku is a rare white peacock who
always wanted to be a dancer in Bollywood."
"That's in Mumbai," said Buddy. "Let's go there."

During their journey, Peggy complained,
"It's too hot to fly."
So they took shelter under a banyan
tree in a village.
"Namaste!" greeted the wise man.
"You need rest. Meditate and you will
feel better. Eat these juicy mangoes too."
Refreshed, the three adventurers
continued their search for Peeku.

"Ooh, dancing!" said Peggy as they arrived in Mumbai.
Monkey and Buddy asked some Bollywood actors if they had seen Peeku.
"Peeku was a star. But he left to learn more from the master of dance in Kerala."
"Peggy, come on! We must leave for Kerala," said Buddy.

They finally reached Kerala and met Peeku's dance master.
"Peeku was an excellent student," he said.
"He is doing a show near the temples of Madurai tonight."

Just in time, Buddy, Peggy and Monkey
made it to the show.

"Look at all these peacocks,"
said Buddy.

"But where is Peeku?"
asked Monkey.

Suddenly, the music began.

Please welcome on stage the fabulous...

...Peeku!

Whizz

Pop

After the show, Peeku hugged Monkey.
"I'm sorry I ran away," said Peeku.
"Though I had a great adventure, I really miss home."
"We'll take you home," said Buddy.
They floated along the River Ganges and celebrated
the Diwali festival of lights on the way.

Monkey and Peeku were happy to be back home in Darjeeling.

Buddy and Peggy were ready for their next adventure.

They waved goodbye as Buddy and Peggy soared above the Himalayas, the highest mountains in the world.

They would never forget their Indian friends.

BUDDY's facts on India

Taj Mahal in Agra is one of the Seven Wonders of the World. It is a marble tomb built by the emperor Shah Jahan in memory of his wife, Mumtaz Mahal.

Jantar Mantar is an ancient observatory in Delhi. The shapes study the movements of the sun, moon and planets. Delhi is the capital city of India.

Tiger is the national animal of India and an endangered species. India has the most wild tigers.

Jaipur has many palaces. At the City Palace is the Peacock Gate. Peacock is the national bird. White peacocks are rare.

Dahanu is home to the indigenous Warli tribe. Warli art portrays village life. The national fruit, mango is also grown there.

Banyan tree is the national tree. The wise man is a yogi, who does yoga and meditates to relax.

Mumbai (Bombay) is India's most populated city. It is the world's largest film producer, Bollywood.

Kerala is one of the states in India. It has coconut tree lined backwaters and sandy beaches.

Kathakali dancers wear face make up. They act using facial expressions and hand gestures.

Madurai is a city famous for the Meenakshi Temple which has 14 intricately carved towers.

River Ganges is the longest river in India. It is a sacred river to Hindus.

Diwali is the Hindu festival of lights. Fireworks are lit to celebrate the victory of good over bad.

Darjeeling has many tea gardens. It is at the foothills of the Himalayas, the highest mountain range in the world.